I'm doomed! I'm just doomed. You see, I really like it here at Tanglewood Academy. So what if we have to wear uniforms? My best friend Jenny goes here, and so does the guy of my dreams—Brett Roberts. I'd just die if I had to go to another school.

But lately my grades have been slipping, and I just can't figure out why. Okay, maybe it could have something to do with all the time I've been spending on writing my new book about different types of boys. Or, it could be all the worrying I've been doing about my friendship with Jenny. You see, lately Jenny has been making me feel like she wants other friends, like I'm not her best friend anymore. She wants to spend all her time with Brianna, this new girl in our car pool, or with Curt, Jenny's new boyfriend. It just doesn't seem fair!

So, now I have three big problems—keeping Jenny as my best friend, getting Brett to notice me, and bringing up my grades so I can stay at Tanglewood. At the rate my problem pile is growing, it will probably reach to the moon in no time!

Just my type

by Karle Dickerson

To Art and Gwyn Doble–
great parent types

Published by Willowisp Press, Inc.
401 E. Wilson Bridge Road, Worthington, Ohio 43085

Copyright ©1989 by Willowisp Press, Inc.

Printed in the United States of America
10 9 8 7 6 5 4 3 2 1

ISBN 0-87406-404-X

One

I shut the school library's dictionary with a sigh and returned to my seat. The dictionary had been no help at all.

"Did you find anything?" hissed Jenny McClain.

It was a few minutes before school started. Jenny (my best friend), Brianna Latham (she's an okay friend, except lately I wonder if she's trying to move in on my best friend), and I were trying to grab some last-minute study time. We were whispering because we were under the glaring eyes of the librarian, Ms. McDowell.

Usually, just the sight of the "Quiet" sign on the librarian's desk was enough to make Jenny and me crack up. But today, for some strange reason, we were trying to follow the rules.

"No, I didn't find anything. I mean, I didn't

find anything that I didn't already know. And I've simply got to find out more about boys—one boy, anyway," I insisted to Jenny under my breath.

"I hate to tell you, but Mr. Kelso isn't going to approve 'boys' as a topic for your social studies paper," Jenny pointed out.

"Why not? We're in the human relations learning module now. And is there anything more interesting to study than boys?" I asked. "I mean, how else are we going to find out anything about them?"

"Look up 'alien creatures' in the subject catalog," whispered Brianna with a noiseless laugh.

"Shhh!" Ms. McDowell cast a disapproving look our way.

I rolled my eyes. Brianna's joke wasn't that funny, but she was right. Boys were definitely alien creatures as far as we were concerned. Jenny, Brianna, and I are in eighth grade, and we've never had a boy so much as look at us. Lately, that's been starting to bug us—a lot. And Jenny and I have been hoping two boys in particular would notice us.

I couldn't figure out why we hadn't had at least one boy look our way in the whole month or so that we'd been back to school. I mean, people tell me I'm not ugly. I look in the mirror and see for myself that I have blond enough

6

hair (although it's too straight), brown eyes, and an okay nose. People say that I can be pretty funny sometimes, too. Jenny has black curly hair and twinkling blue eyes. Brianna has a great figure since she's a swimmer. She also has nice clothes because her mom owns Tres Chic Juniors, a trendy clothing boutique at the mall.

No, I couldn't figure out why the guys stay away from us in globs. I couldn't even find a good book on the subject.

"I wish someone would write a book about boys," I said, doodling in the margin of a fresh sheet of paper. "At least someone could write a book that would tell me if Brett Roberts is my type. He seems to be. Still, you can get fooled. I wish someone would just write a good book about boys, about *types* of boys."

Jenny frowned at me. "Don't get any ideas. How many books have you started to write, but never finished? Besides, not all boys can be classified by types, you know. Some boys are just regular people."

I shook my head at Jenny. She's my best friend, but sometimes she just doesn't seem to understand me. And one thing she doesn't understand is my plan to be a world-famous author someday. And another thing she doesn't understand about me is how I classify people by types. Jenny says that there are all kinds of people in the world and that they can't always be put into neat little categories. She doesn't understand that identifying types of people helps me to deal with them better.

She is right about one thing, though. I never seem to get very far with any of my books. Maybe that's because I never can seem to stay interested in any one thing for very long. But, wait a minute. I had been interested in boys for a while. And I had been interested in Brett for a particularly long time. *Hmm, maybe I should write a book about boys,* I thought. My thoughts started racing. I grabbed a pencil and wrote on a piece of paper:

Boys. They're one thing girls can't know enough about. Just running into one (especially a cute one) in the hall is enough to make most girls' stomachs do wheelies. But why? After all, a boy is just a boy—even if there are all types of boys. There are Cute Types, Handsome Types, and Super Good-Looking Types.

Boy, that sounded dumb. *And which type is Brett?* I wondered. I stopped writing and thought about him while I chewed the tip of my pencil. *If only I could figure out what type he is*, I thought. I sighed and closed my notebook.

Jenny shook her head and then pulled a

newspaper clipping out of her notebook. "Well, that's enough about boys. I've got to write up the summary for my current event for today. Look at this," she whispered. She pointed at the picture she'd clipped of some hungry-looking people holding out tin plates for food.

"Drought victims line up for food distribution," the caption read.

"My current event isn't nearly that sad. Why do you always pick the saddest ones?" I asked impatiently.

Jenny is the type who always rescues kittens that are stuck up in trees, and who wheels stray shopping carts back to supermarkets. Don't get me wrong. I like the idea of helping others, but sometimes Jenny carries things too far.

"I wish we could do something about it," Jenny said as she started writing. "Those people look so...hungry. Hey, look. There's an address in the article that tells you how to send donations for food and blankets."

Just then the bell rang. It was time to go to first period.

"Well, we'd better go," Jenny said as she put away her half-written summary. She opened her purse and applied a little clear lip gloss—the only kind we're allowed to wear at our strict private school. "I get my math test back today. I hope I got an *A*."

I combed my stick-straight blond hair and reclipped my tortoiseshell banana clip. "I get my science test back today. I hope I passed," I whispered.

Jenny smiled. "You will. You're the brains of this group, the straight-*A* kid."

"Not anymore," I said mournfully. "My brilliance seems to have short-circuited lately."

We headed out the library door together, and then we parted ways. I walked alone to my science class, since Jenny and Brianna went the opposite way to their first class. While I walked, I tried not to think about my grades, which were really taking a nosedive lately. I wasn't sure why. Maybe it was because I had so much on my mind.

When Mr. Hogg handed back our science tests, I knew I was doomed. No, I mean really doomed. It was easy to see by the way Mr. Hogg furrowed his brow as he came marching down my aisle. He stopped right beside my desk and let out a sigh that made me feel like I had had one last chance to save the planet from destruction, but I'd decided to go play a video game instead.

"I see that you chose not to study, Miss Ferris," Mr. Hogg said sorrowfully.

Mr. Hogg always calls his eighth graders

"mister" and "miss." He says that if he treats us like adults, we will act like adults. I could have told him it doesn't work. I mean, the kids at Tanglewood Academy still call him "Mr. Hog" behind his back and oink like pigs when he walks by. That doesn't sound very adult to me.

By now everybody in the whole class was looking at me—including Sherri Shepherd, The Cute, Bouncy Adorable Type, who is always the teacher's pet. I took one look at her smug face, and I knew my face was reddening like an overblown poppy. My mind started working feverishly.

"Oh, no, Mr. Hogg," I began, the gears in my brain starting to warm up. "It wasn't that I chose not to study. Actually, I started to study very hard for all my classes—English, science, and social studies. And my dad always says that brains work like..."

I paused for inspiration. I looked across the aisle at Wendell Porter, The Math and Total Nerd Type. Wendell is a complete computer freak. I had found my inspiration.

I plunged on. "...computers. Well, I think I must have had so many facts and dates and places all stuffed into my data banks that I hit memory overload. By the time I came to class, everything went kaput! My mental disks were shot." I took a deep breath and waited for Mr. Hogg's reaction.

Mr. Hogg just looked at me, shook his head, and smiled his first smile of the day. "Miss Ferris, if you would work half as hard studying for your tests as you do coming up with fantastic stories about your brain's hitting memory overload, I think you might be able to salvage your grade in this class," he said, handing my paper to me. "Remember, one thing we stress at Tanglewood Academy is academic excellence."

I took one look at the big red *D* scribbled across my paper, and my ears started roaring so loudly that I barely heard the class laughing. I'd never gotten a *D* on a test before. When my parents saw this, my data banks *were* going to be overloaded with something, my parents' disappointment. Mom's the head nurse at Beachside Community Hospital. Dad's a property manager for a bunch of big office buildings all over California. Both of them are big on doing only a few things, but doing them well.

"Tanglewood seems to be too much pressure for you. Maybe you should transfer to the public school," my parents would say.

Then I'd be doomed because Jenny would still go to Tanglewood. And so would Brett Roberts (The Mystery Guy Type!) and some of the cutest guys that our creepy southern

California beach town has to offer. But don't tell anyone about all this. That stuff about Brett is top secret.

"Wow! You got a *D*, Cathy?" asked Jenny as we met at nutrition break after history class. "What's going on with you lately? You always got good grades before. And you like science. What happened?"

I didn't even try the memory overload excuse on Jenny. She's known me for too long. We've been friends ever since my family moved to Beachside last year. Jenny was the first person I met at Tanglewood Academy.

"I don't know," I said and shrugged as we walked up to the snack line. I did suspect that my bad grades had something to do with the fact that I was trying to do too many things at once. There's school and piano lessons. And Jenny and I had started a dog-washing business to earn some spending money. And then there are boys. And writing books. "I guess it was because I stayed up the night before the test and started writing a new book instead of studying."

"You and your books," Jenny said, tucking her rich chestnut hair behind her ears and adjusting her purse on her shoulder. "Why do you write those silly old things, anyway?"

"Silly old things?" I puffed up like a water balloon that was ready to explode all over the place. "My books are not silly old things. I'm going to sell them when I grow up and become a world-famous author. I'll be rich, and then you can borrow money from me," I finished triumphantly.

"There's one problem," said my best friend as we inched our way up toward the front of the line. "You never finish writing any of the books that you start. You'll never be rich and famous that way."

"Can I borrow 50 cents?" I asked, ignoring Jenny's comment. We were now at the window where you order your snack, and a quick search of the pocket of my regulation gray jumper told me I was anything but rich that day.

"Sure," Jenny said with a sigh, handing me two quarters. "That makes a total of about $200 you owe me now."

"That's not true," I protested hotly, taking the quarter and ordering a bran muffin. "And, anyway, I can pay you back this Saturday after we get our dog-washing money."

"Okay," said Jenny good-naturedly. She ordered her muffin. "I have a great idea for how we can help those hungry people."

"How?" I mumbled disinterestedly, my mouth full of muffin.

"Let's donate the money from our dog-washing business to the hungry people,"

Jenny said enthusiastically.

Jenny and I started our dog-washing business last summer to earn extra pocket money. Already we have a steady stream of neighborhood customers. And Brianna hates dogs. So, that's one thing I do with Jenny that she can't horn in on.

"I can't," I said, shaking my head. "If I did that, I'd never be able to pay you back!"

"Whatever," Jenny said with a shrug. "But I'm going to donate my half of the money. Oh, and I forgot to tell you. Mrs. Roberts called my mom and said she wants us to wash her dogs this Saturday," Jenny added. "That should bring in extra money."

"Oh, you *forgot* to tell me?" I asked, gripping her arm. I mean, this was front-page news. Mrs. Roberts is Brett Roberts' mom. My boy-oh-boy alarm was ringing in my ears.

Jenny turned a knowing eye on me. "Well, I didn't think it was that big of a deal. After all, Mrs. Roberts isn't Brett, and besides— EEK! Look! He's walking toward us right now."

I stopped mid-muffin munch, and my eyes darted around until they rested on The Cute Type himself. *Or, is he The Tall, Dark, Athletic, Handsome type*? I wondered. I shook my head. This was confusing. He was walking toward us, but he didn't look our way. He's in my social studies class, but he hardly knew I existed. And Jenny had been talking so loudly that I was positive he'd heard her.

"Come on," I squeaked, dropping crumbs everywhere and tugging on Jenny's blue blazer. "Let's get out of here. He had to have heard you. I think I'm going to swoon right here!"

"Swoon?" laughed Jenny, allowing me to lead her away by the sleeve of her blazer. "People don't swoon anymore, even if they do happen to be within hearing distance of their biggest crush. Only heroines in romance novels swoon."

"You'd try to swoon if it was Curt Millikin who'd overheard you talking about him," I said when we were safe and out of Brett range. Jenny teased me about my crush, so I could tease her about hers.

From a safe distance, I watched Brett get into the snack line. Then I took a big eyeful of his broad, muscular shoulders encased in the school uniform, which is a dark blue blazer. So what if everyone in the school wears one? On Brett, it looks great. He has dark, almost blue-black hair and perfectly blue eyes. Blue is definitely his color. Come to think of it, any color is Brett's color.

I couldn't figure out why one minute I was madly in like with him, and the next minute—

like just then, when he started talking to Sherri Shepherd—I couldn't stand him. That was one more thing I'd have to learn about guys. How can they make your head ache and your heart pound all in the same millisecond?

Jenny watched me watch him. She wrinkled her nose and took a bite of her muffin. "Mmmph," was all she said.

Then she grabbed the corner of my science test sticking out of my notebook and looked at the big *D* scrawled angrily across it.

"What's this going to do to your science grade?" she asked, her blue eyes looking sorrowfully at me, the way Mr. Hogg's eyes had only a little while ago.

"I'll give you three guesses," I said, taking the last bite of my muffin. Suddenly, I could feel the muffin sitting heavily in my stomach. "If I don't get serious and bring my grades up in a hurry, I could be saying good-bye to dear old Tanglewood Academy."

"Your parents would freak," Jenny announced to me like—duh—I didn't already know that.

"You're telling me," I muttered, licking my fingers and wishing my stomach didn't suddenly feel like it was staging the Bran Muffin Rebellion. "I'd freak, too. I mean, what would I do if I had to transfer to another school and be there without you?"

Jenny looked at me with alarm in her big dark eyes. "Well, school definitely wouldn't be as much fun for me. But you'd survive and make some new friends, I guess. That would be good. And at least we'd still live near each other."

"I don't want new friends," I said quickly. Why did Jenny make me feel like she wanted other friends lately? Wasn't I good enough? Last year, we did everything together—just the two of us. This year, it's different somehow, like we were growing apart from each other. "Anyway, I'll get my grades back up."

"Good. Because I couldn't stand it if you went to another school," Jenny said simply. "You're my best friend."

She fingered her half of the heart-shaped pendant we bought together. The half that she wears says "best." I have the other half that says "friends."

I like it when Jenny says that I'm her best friend. I sure don't like it that more and more these days, she's hanging out with Brianna and suggesting that we both expand our circle of friends. Sure, people need other friends. But I was worried that Jenny was seriously shopping for another best friend. I've never been The Sharing Type. Just ask my mom!

Two

MY day went from bad to worse. Right before lunch, I got back my English essay. Ms. Perry had scrawled a glaring red *C* across it.

"You have fine ideas, but the essay lacks organization. The topic strays," she wrote at the top.

I sighed. I'd been so proud of my essay. We'd read a short story about a boy who'd been caught cheating on his finals and was expelled from school. I'd written that I thought the boy shouldn't have cheated, but that he should have been given a second chance, too. Then I'd written this great story about what happened when the boy left school and decided to be a rock star instead.

Even if Ms. Perry didn't think I could write, I knew I was a born author.

"Cathy, why haven't you opened your grammar book like the rest of the class?" Ms.

Perry asked as she passed my desk.

I wanted to say, *Because I hate grammar. It makes me certifiably insane.* But I opened my textbook and tried not to distract myself by looking at Brett, who was seated three chairs in front of me.

We were just getting into adjectives when I noticed Jenny and Curt passing notes across the aisle to each other. I didn't know Curt very well, but I had to admit that he was The Major-League Cute Type. But then again, he hangs out with Sherri Shepherd quite a bit. Anyone who hangs out with Sherri has to be The Jerk Type.

Jenny disagreed with me.

"People can be very different from their friends," she'd said the last time I'd brought up the subject. "Anyway, Sherri can't be that bad—not once you get to know her."

What did I tell you? Jenny's got a heart that's softer than a marshmallow.

I watched Jenny giggle at one of the notes Curt passed her. When Ms. Perry called on me and asked me to name three adjectives, I almost didn't have to think. I answered, "Mushy, gushy, and gross."

The entire class thought it was funny, but Ms. Perry frowned.

Later, Jenny and I walked to gym class

together and suited up for our touch football game. And she didn't tell me what Curt had said in his note. It's stuff like this that was starting to bother me. More and more, Jenny seemed to be keeping little things from me.

After school, Jenny and I walked to the locker we shared. I was just about to ask her if she wanted to come over and do homework together when Brianna came racing up and started babbling. They started talking about Curt.

While they talked, I stood there feeling really left out. I'd read somewhere that authors are the kind of people who stand on the sidelines and watch people. But watching Jenny and Brianna didn't make me feel better.

After a minute, Jenny must have noticed how I was feeling because she turned to me. "So, that's it. I have to get Curt to ask me to the dance. Will you help me?" she asked.

"What dance?" I asked.

"Weren't you listening? There's going to be an eighth-grade dance!" Brianna exclaimed. "We just had it approved at the student government meeting this afternoon. It will be Tanglewood's first ever eighth-grade dance."

Jenny looked at Brianna like she was some kind of hero just because she was in student government and had gotten a dance approved. Big hairy deal. I fiddled with my necklace.

"Now that you mention it, I don't see what you see in Curt," I said to Jenny, just to bug her. "He's not your type at all."

"He's cute, and he's funny," Jenny said. "You should have seen the cartoon he drew of Ms. Perry. Anyway, how do you know he's not my type?"

"I think he's cute, too," Brianna said, defending Jenny.

Who cares what you think? my brain shouted at Brianna.

The three of us headed down the hall to the front of the school where we waited for our car pool. It used to be only Jenny and I in the car pool. But this year Brianna and another girl named Lacy Watkins had joined it. I liked it better the old way.

While we waited for Mrs. Latham, Brianna continued talking about how cute Curt was until I almost wanted to barf.

"Curt may be cute and funny, but he's not your type," I jumped in again when Brianna stopped for a breath. "Now don't get upset," I said, seeing the look of anger creeping onto Jenny's face. "After all, I am your best friend. And I should protect you from guy types that you should stay away from."

Jenny hooted. And when she hooted, everyone knew it. She threw her head back and made this loud, weird noise. I hated it when she hooted. And I especially hated it when she hooted at me.

"What are you hooting at?" I asked.

"You," she said. "You act like you know so much about guys. And you've never even been on a date or anything."

"So what. Neither have you," I replied.

Luckily, Lacy Watkins came up just then, or Jenny, Brianna, and I probably would have ended up in a three-way quarrel. Not that having a quarrel would have been a big deal, since Jenny and I argue at least once a day. And we usually get over our arguments in a hurry. But now that Brianna was involved, it could get stickier.

On the way home, everyone talked about the dance. I tuned out and thought about my book again. I wondered if anyone had ever written a book on guy types. Probably not.

I was sure it would be a best-seller. Every girl in every school across the United States would be dying to get her hands on my book! I closed my eyes and imagined the glory. Talk about fame and fortune! And maybe Brett would notice me then. Aren't guys attracted to The Rich and Famous Type?

A poke in the ribs startled me out of my rosy daydream. "We're at your house, Cathy," Brianna said as we pulled up to the curb in front of my house.

I tucked my books under my arm and opened the car door. "Thanks, Mrs. Latham," I called over my shoulder.

The car took off, and the future world-famous author turned to walk up the sidewalk. My feet dragged. Usually our cozy, weather-worn beach house seemed ready to fold me up in its arms, but that day it felt like sea-weed, waiting to trap me. I wasn't looking forward to showing my mom my science test— or my English essay.

I opened the front door and plopped my books on the hall table.

"Mom, I'm home," I called, but not too loudly.

Then I made a beeline for my room so Mom couldn't ask me how my day had been. I was very willing to wait to show her my poor grades on my papers. Anyway, I was dying to grab my notebook and start writing my newest book. And I already knew how it would start.

This book is dedicated to girls everywhere who want to know about boys. They are hard to understand, and that's why I am going to write a whole book about different guy types.

I didn't have a chance to get much down on paper before my nine-year-old sister, Amy, came galloping into my room. She was wearing her soccer uniform and eating a chocolate cookie. Her jersey and her face were all smeared with chocolate. Amy's The Little Sister Creep Type.

"Guess what? I kicked three goals today," Amy said, licking her fingers.

"That's gross," I said, looking at her messy face disgustedly. "Get out of here, and go wash your face."

"You always tell me to get out of here," Amy complained.

"That's because you're always bugging me," I grumbled. "Put down my stuffed giraffe. Don't you dare touch anything in my room. I mean it."

Amy's always playing with my stuffed jungle animal collection. She has her own stuff. Why doesn't she leave my stuff alone?

"Guess what?" Amy asked gleefully as she threw the giraffe on my bed. "One of your teachers called and wanted to talk to Mom."

I looked quickly at her, but then I pretended it was no big deal.

"So what?" I shrugged. "Now, go away."

"Mom looked angry," Amy added, watching me to see if I was going to squirm.

Just then, Mom's voice came floating up the stairs. "Catherine, come down here. We need to talk."

"Ha, ha," said Amy. "I told you! She called you Catherine. You're going to get into trouble."

She started doing a little victory dance. Of all the sisters in the world, Amy's the worst. I reached out and tugged hard on one of her reddish-blond pigtails.

"You little creep," I hissed. "I'm coming, Mom," I said in a much sweeter voice.

One thing I'd learned in the 13 years that I'd lived with Mom and Dad is that problems only become worse if I act angry and sulk when I get into trouble.

I walked slowly to the kitchen where Mom was stirring something on the stove. I sniffed the air appreciatively.

Mom stirred thoughtfully for a moment.

"I got a phone call today, Catherine," she said calmly.

I froze for a moment. Then I decided to quickly change the subject.

I inhaled the aroma of the contents of the pot. "Mmm. This smells great," I said cheerfully, as if I hadn't heard her. "What is it?"

Mom laughed, and then she frowned

slightly and shook her head. "It's a seafood recipe. And don't try to change the subject, Cathy."

I looked at her in innocent surprise.

"You got a phone call?" I asked. "That's nice. It's nice to get phone calls. I'll bet you get lonely here in the afternoons before I get home and—"

"Catherine," Mom said sternly. "The call was from one of your teachers."

"It's not my fault Ms. Perry gave me a *C* in English," I interrupted.

"Ah, so you're having a problem in English, too?" Mom asked. "The phone call was from Mr. Hogg. He was very concerned about a recent science test you took."

"I can explain," I said quickly. "I think my brain went on overload because we had so many tests and quizzes last week."

Mom pursed her lips and then picked a piece of lint off my blazer.

"Honey," she said quietly. "Your father and I have been concerned for a while that you might be taking on too much. You have your piano lessons and your dog-washing thing with Jenny. And you have a very strict school program on top of all that. Maybe Tanglewood is too much pressure for you. Maybe you'd be better off in another school."

27

I panicked. Visions of attending the public school, Jennyless, floated before my eyes.

"No, honestly, it's not any pressure at all," I babbled. "I'll study harder. Really, I will."

Mom shrugged. "I think you're going to have to give up some of your extra activities—like the dog-washing business, for instance."

"No, don't ask me to give up that," I said. I panicked. "I can't give up the dog-washing business. That's the only thing left that Jenny and I can do without Brianna butting in. She hates dogs, and I'm glad."

"Oh, Cathy, Brianna seems like a nice girl. Can't you stretch a little to include her, too?" Mom asked.

"Besides, I like dogs," I babbled on, ignoring her question. "And since you and Amy are allergic to them, and we can't have one—" My voice trailed off.

One look at Mom's face told me she wasn't convinced.

"Well, you're going to have to do something," Mom said. "You're the one who has to manage your time. Your dad and I are very proud of your achievements, but we don't want you spreading yourself too thin.

"I can't give up the dog-washing thing," I protested.

Mom went on. "I'll let you handle it for now,

but make an effort to bring up your grades. Once your dad finds out about this, he'll insist you make some changes. Now, set the table, and then practice your piano."

A few minutes later, I was seated at the piano, bashing out some finger exercises. My mind wasn't on the keyboard at all. I was listening to the waves crashing onto the beach outside and picturing myself getting kicked out of Tanglewood, never to see Brett or Jenny again. And then I worried about how I was going to bring up my grades in a hurry so all of that wouldn't happen.

My fingers traveled over the *E* key that was always flat, no matter how many times we had the piano tuned. I winced. I had to remember to stay away from that key if possible. That led me to thinking about my newest book some more. How would I get material to write about? Guy types mostly stay away from me.

I wrote in my head:

There are all types of guys—some cute ones and even some very cute ones. Unfortunately, there are also Geek Supremo and Jerk Types. Stay away from these types. And warn your best friend to stay away from them, too.

My fingers came crashing down on the keyboard as I started pounding out my first practice piece.

Three

IT was Saturday morning, and I was trying to grab the last few peaceful minutes of sleep before the weekly housecleaning began. The sun was streaming through my blinds onto my bed, and already I could hear commotion going on downstairs. My parents start early on the housecleaning on Saturdays.

I wanted to snuggle under the covers and think about Brett. With my eyes closed, I mentally pictured Brett asking me to the eighth-grade dance. In my daydream, I tossed my blond hair back casually and said, "Why, yes. Of course, I'd love to go to the dance with you, Brett," with total cool.

But just as he reached out to hold my hand, Amy threw open my bedroom door, and kaput! There went my great daydream. I knew there would be no more sleeping or daydreaming this morning.

"Don't you ever knock?" I asked grumpily. "And why can't you ever sleep in?"

"Sleep in?" Amy asked, blinking. Her pajama top was riding up and so was one leg of her pajama bottoms. Her hair was wild and messy from sleeping. "Are you kidding? Then I'd miss Saturday morning cartoons! Are you coming?" she asked.

"No," I grumbled. "Go away."

I'd learned that the best way to deal with Amy was to stay away from her as much as possible. After she left, I stuck out my tongue. Then I threw back the covers and sprawled there for a moment. Finally, I got up and called Jenny to find out when she'd be coming over.

"Are you up?" I asked when Jenny answered.

"Yeah," she said. "My mom's taking me to the store to pick up some more flea shampoo, and then I'll be right over."

"Okay," I said with a yawn. "Take your time."

Jenny was The Early-Bird Type, and I definitely was not. I slowly took a shower, and then I changed into my oldest jeans, an old sweatshirt, and old tennis shoes. After straightening my room and arranging my stuffed jungle animals on my bed, I went downstairs to have something to eat.

Mom already had the vacuum going in the living room. Dad was in the front yard attacking the lawn with a weed whacker. Over all the noise, I could hear the blare of Amy's cartoons on the TV. I gave Mom a good-morning kiss. She ruffled my hair and continued vacuuming.

By the time I ate and went to the garage to pull out the dog-washing signs, Jenny was wheeling up the driveway on her beat-up beach bicycle. She puffed and pushed back her dark sweaty bangs.

"Hi!" she said, unhooking a plastic grocery bag from her handlebars. "I got a huge bottle of Super Rid Fleez."

"Good," I said, eyeing the bottle that she held up. "Because here comes Mr. Madison and his Saint Bernard. Brandy's coat is always filled with fleas."

"Oh, no," groaned Jenny. "I can't handle that dog first thing in the morning. He's so huge."

"Yeah, well, at least he likes the water," I said with a sigh as I tacked up the signs on the side of the house near the hose and tub. Mr. Madison is our next-door neighbor, and one of our regular customers. "And, remember, big dogs mean that we earn big bucks.

Think of the new Bloated Robots tape that you can buy with the money you earn from washing Brandy."

"You forget. I can't buy new tapes or records. I'm donating this week's earnings to the hungry people," Jenny said.

I shrugged. "Not that again. Well, then Brandy's money can help buy lots of food for the hungry people."

Jenny cheered up at that idea. We charged two dollars for small dogs, three dollars for medium-size dogs, and four dollars for big dogs. Brandy is definitely in the big-dog category. Mr. Madison usually tips us generously, too. Jenny waved to Mr. Madison and started filling the tub for the humongous dog.

"And be sure to get all the soap out," Mr. Madison said crisply. "Last time, he scratched for three days because of the leftover soap in his fur."

"Yes, Mr. Madison," we both said.

We started lathering up the big slobbering dog while Mr. Madison sat on the bench under the tree by the front walk. Brandy licked our faces and wagged his tail enthusiastically, fanning water all over us.

Jenny and I were a good team. After all, we'd been open for business practically every weekend since the beginning of summer. Now that it was fall, we knew there wouldn't be too many warm weekends left. Then we'd have to close up business for the winter.

I soaked Brandy with the hose. Jenny applied the shampoo while I scrubbed his thick coat. Then we rinsed Brandy thoroughly under his owner's watchful eye. We stood back while Brandy shook himself mightily, and then we dried him off. At last, we were finished, and Brandy was sweet-smelling and clean. Mr. Madison handed us our money, as well as a nice tip.

"This ought to help feed some hungry people," Jenny said happily. She beamed as she put the crumpled money in the shoe box that we'd placed on the washing machine.

Business was brisk that morning, but I kept an eye out for Mrs. Roberts. I half-closed my eyes while I soaped doggie bodies and pictured her raving about me to Brett.

"Those girls are unbelievable. You really ought to ask Cathy to go to the eighth-grade dance with you, Brett," she'd say.

Then I sighed. Leave it to an author to come up with a storybook ending.

By late morning, my clothes were damp and covered with hair of an amazing variety of colors. My own hair was all over the place. I was sweaty and cranky. So was Jenny.

Suddenly, Jenny grabbed my sleeve. "Don't look now, but here comes Mr. Wonderful."

"Oh, no!" I wailed. "Look at me."

Jenny did. Then she hooted.

Brett came walking up the driveway looking cool and wearing a pair of khaki pants and a royal blue polo shirt. I sucked in my breath and wished feverishly for a magic genie to appear and make me look presentable. But I had no such luck. I was doomed.

"Hi," Brett said, scarcely noticing us. He looked past both Jenny and me and was checking out the basketball hoop that Dad had attached to our garage years ago. Brett's two large German shepherds strained against their leashes.

"Hi, Brett," Jenny said when I didn't say anything. "I thought your mom was going to bring Trapper and Bongo to be washed."

"She was, but I got stuck doing it," Brett said. He didn't sound too happy about it. "Now I'm going to miss practice today."

"Oh, gee, that's too bad," Jenny sympathized.

"Uh, yeah," I managed to croak out, wondering what kind of practice Brett was talking about. I knew Brett played football for Tanglewood, and I knew he was on some other sports teams, too. I gripped my scrub brush tightly as I looked at Brett's gorgeous face. I tried not to notice that my heart was pounding out a rap beat.

"I really wanted to go, too," Brett went on.

"What a shame," Jenny, the marshmallow heart, said.

"It really is," Brett said. "The guys need me."

What was the big deal about missing one little practice? I thought.

"Uh, well, bring on the dogs," I said with a forced laugh. "It's time for a bath, Trapper. You, too, Bongo."

Brett tossed the leashes to me disinterestedly. I caught them both expertly. Brett didn't even notice.

"Do you have a basketball anywhere?" he asked.

"No, but there's a volleyball in the garage," I said as Jenny started to fill up the tub.

It was just my luck that Brett would come over when I wasn't expecting him. And I had to look even worse than the dogs we were bathing. No wonder he preferred to toss around a stupid ball.

I dragged Trapper over by the hose after I tied Bongo to the tree to wait his turn. Trapper was less than pleased about the prospect of a bath. I grabbed him by the neck.

He sat down hard and put on the brakes.

"Help me, Jenny," I said between gritted teeth.

Out of the corner of one eye, I saw that Brett had found our old volleyball. He had started shooting baskets.

"Athletic Types," I whispered to Jenny. "They have one-track minds. They don't realize anyone around them even exists."

"You're just upset because he's not paying attention to you," Jenny gasped as we lifted Trapper into the tub.

"I am not."

While we got Trapper all full of suds, I was seized with inspiration. The first chapter of my book would be about Athletic Types. Of course, I would have to get to know Brett better so I could write about this type.

It was hard to think about my book and hold Trapper for his bath at the same time. Jenny and I fought and wrestled with the oversized pooch right to the bitter end, all the while accompanied by the nonstop *plump—plump* of the volleyball.

"The least he could do is help," Jenny whispered to me. She tied Trapper to the tree, and then she grabbed Bongo and turned him over to me.

But Bongo was smarter than Trapper. Or,

maybe he just hated baths even more than Trapper did—if that was possible. I reached for his collar and missed. Bongo shot down the driveway.

"Oh, no!" Jenny gasped.

"You're telling me," I said as I spun around and watched Bongo sail merrily into the street.

"Bongo!" shouted Brett, dropping the ball and breaking into a run. "Help me catch him!" he yelled at me as he ran past.

I didn't need a second invitation.

"Stay with Trapper," I gasped at Jenny as I bounded after Brett.

Bongo was rapidly disappearing. Suddenly, I spied Sherri Shepherd and two of her friends coming down the street toward us. She didn't even notice when Bongo shot past her.

"Oh, great," I moaned. Now Sherri is going to be witness to the biggest mistake of my life.

"Hi, Brett," she cooed, tossing her glimmering hair as Brett tore past her.

"Are you chasing after Brett again, Cathy?" she asked as I ran toward her.

I slowed down for a second.

"Brett's dog got away, and we have to catch him," I babbled.

"Sure," Sherri, The Jerk Type, said.

I looked up again and saw that Bongo and Brett were headed for Peninsula Boulevard. The street was filled with traffic. What if Bongo runs out in front of a car? Without another thought about Sherri, I took off running again.

Bongo ran right into the middle of the boulevard, dodging traffic. Cars screeched as he crossed into their lanes. Horns beeped. I closed my eyes and jammed my fists into my mouth. I was sure that any minute I was going to hear a sickening *thud*.

"Quick! Press the Walk light! I think he's across," came Brett's voice.

I opened my eyes and breathed a sigh of relief. Bongo was safe.

"Hey, dude, are you tryin' to kill your dog?" one surfer-looking guy shouted at Brett.

It seemed like forever until the light changed to green. We both ran as fast as we could and finally caught up with Bongo by the fire station.

"Bad dog," Brett said sternly as he snatched up the leash. Bongo wasn't the least bit sorry he'd almost been killed. But I sure was.

"I'm so sorry, Brett," I gasped out when I could talk.

Brett looked at me without saying anything.

He didn't have to say anything. I knew what he was thinking. He was thinking that I was the stupidest girl in the world.

We walked up the street in silence. I was miserable. Not only was I feeling bad because I'd nearly lost a customer's dog, but it was Brett's dog at that.

I replayed the scene over and over in my head that night in my room. I'd blown my one and only chance with Brett.

Well, boys are jerks, anyway—especially The Insensitive Jock Types like Brett, who wouldn't even let a girl make an honest mistake.

Stay away from The Insensitive Jock Type.
I'd write that in my book.

A-ha! That was it! I'd title my book *Guy Types to Stay Away From*. It would have a huge skull and crossbones on the cover like they put on poison labels. My book will warn every girl in America about the types of guys to stay away from.

And Brett would be the subject of my first chapter of *Guy Types to Stay Away From!*

Four

O N Monday, I learned just how fast news can spread around a school. Practically everyone at Tanglewood had heard that I'd almost gotten Brett's dog killed. It's funny. I never would have pegged Brett as The Blabbermouth Type.

Oh, well, I thought dismally. *I've always heard an author's life is lonely.* At least I had more material for my book. I could start a new chapter on The Blabbermouth Type.

Stay away from The Blabbermouth Type, I wrote furiously during science class when we were supposed to be correcting our homework papers. *These guys don't let you make even the smallest mistake without spreading it all over school.*

I pressed down so hard on my paper that my pencil snapped. I thought no one had noticed. But I was wrong.

"Miss Ferris, what are you doing?" Mr. Hogg demanded.

"Nothing," I said, slamming my notebook closed.

Mr. Hogg continued glaring at me. "I thought a phone call home would be enough to convince you that you need to get serious about this class. What's more important than bringing up your grade?"

Writing my best-seller about boys, I said silently to myself. I pictured what would happen if I told Mr. Hogg that. Then I made a noise like a sick turkey while I tried not to giggle.

"I suggest you pay attention to your class-work, Miss Ferris," Mr. Hogg said as he moved on with the lesson. "You do want to pass science this year, don't you?"

That comment brought me back to reality. I had better figure out a way to do what Mr. Hogg suggested—in a hurry. So, I made heroic efforts to concentrate on the microscopic beasts under my microscope while Sherri smiled sideways at me and whispered to everyone within range.

After class was over, I walked slowly toward our table by the snack bar.

"Hi, Jen," I said. Boy, did I need a friend just then.

Jenny sat on the table and pulled off her blazer. She set it in a heap on top of her books.

"I have some bad news." She was watching my face closely. "I guess you know everyone's heard about Brett's dog and how you nearly–"

"I know. Can you believe what a blabbermouth Brett is?" I asked with an impatient wave of my hand. "Boy, did I choose the wrong type of guy to have a crush on, or what?"

Jenny stopped. "Not necessarily," she said. "How do you know it was Brett who told everyone? You don't know Brett all that well, anyway. How can you type him?"

"I don't need to know people that well to know what they're like," I answered.

"You're always lumping people into types, Cathy. You really can't do that."

"Why not?" I asked as we got in line at the snack bar.

"People are too complicated to put them into one category. You can't just say they're this or that type and write them off," Jenny pointed out.

"Oh, yeah?" I muttered.

I thought about Brett, The Blabbermouth Type. Or, was he just The Insensitive Jock Type? Well, he was a type, anyway.

We got to the front of the line and ordered orange juice and cheese bread. Jenny waved at Brianna and some other girls who were sitting on a picnic bench by the gymnasium. I tried to steer Jenny over to a different picnic table, but Brianna motioned us over to sit with them.

"Come on," she said and walked toward the picnic bench. I sighed and followed.

"You know, Sherri came up to me this morning and told me that Brett's still really upset about Bongo," Brianna said, looking at me as I sat down on the bench.

"Yeah, everybody was talking about it in gym class," said Lacy Watkins.

I ran my hand through my hair and adjusted my barrette.

"You're telling me. I swear, everyone's heard the story by now," I said. "When I see him in social studies class, I'm going to give Mr. Brett Roberts a piece of my mind."

The other girls turned their attention to an article in a fan magazine.

"Wait," Jenny said to me in a low voice. "You can't give Brett a piece of your mind. You have a major-league crush on him."

"I *had* a major-league crush on him. That's past tense," I insisted and took a big bite out of my cheese bread.

Suddenly, I felt someone squeeze in next to me on the picnic bench. I looked up and with a shock realized it was Brett. The bite of bread in my mouth suddenly seemed three sizes bigger than it was, and my tongue went dry. Had he heard me?

"Hi," he said, plopping down his books.

I swallowed my bite in one gulp. I could feel it travel all the way down my esophagus and land with a *thud* in my stomach.

Brett's blazer sleeve touched mine, and I felt something like an electric shock run through me. I fiddled nervously with my barrette.

"Hi, Brett," Jenny said uneasily.

Brett turned to me then. "I just wanted to say that I'm sorry if I seemed all angry about Bongo, but I was so scared he'd get run over when he ran across Peninsula Boulevard," Brett said.

I nearly went into shock. Brett was apologizing to me? This was no way for an Insensitive Jock Type to act.

"And another thing," he went on. "I didn't want you to think I was the one who spread it all over school."

"Oh, yeah? Then who did?" I suddenly exploded. I couldn't help it. The whole thing made me furious. After all, Bongo's escape hadn't been all my fault. He'd been a difficult dog to begin with. I hadn't meant to let him squirm out of my arms. And Brett had acted like I'd done it on purpose. Sure, Brett is cute. But that doesn't mean he can get away with just anything.

Brett seemed uncomfortable as he realized that every girl at our table was looking at us. Suddenly, he jumped up.

"Well, that's all I wanted to say. I'll see you in social studies," he said. Then he walked off.

Jenny and I looked at each other.

"That was weird," she said. "You shouldn't have been so snappy about it. He was trying to apologize to you."

"Yeah, now that he's done the damage and it's all over school, he's trying to apologize. And what's worse is that he's saying he didn't tell everyone," I said.

"Frankly, I think it was Sherri who spread the news all over school," Jenny whispered to me. "Maybe you're right. Maybe she's a real Jerk Type."

"I still think it was Brett," I said.

Boys are weird, I wrote in my notebook during math class later that day. *Don't let them throw you off. They may come and apologize after they've blabbed your mistake all over school. But they're probably just doing it so everyone in school will think they're*

Everybody's Friend Types, but they're not.

Then I slammed my notebook shut and tried not to notice that Jenny and Brianna were laughing together—a lot.

Later that day, I slid into my seat in social studies. As Brett came into the room, I looked down at my book and started doodling on the cover. Maybe I could transfer out of social studies so I'd never have to see Brett again. Of course, if I got kicked out of Tanglewood...

Mr. Kelso stood up when the bell rang and started to call roll. When he finished, he said, "Today, class, we are going to discuss the projects we are going to present at back-to-school night."

I slid down in my seat. Uh-oh. I'd forgotten about back-to-school night. Mom and Dad are going to have time to talk to all of my teachers and to find out how badly I've been doing in school. I was really doomed.

Mr. Kelso talked on and on while I envisioned myself being escorted off Tanglewood's campus. I pictured myself eating lunch by myself at some nameless new school. Then, to torture myself big time, I pictured Jenny and Brianna wearing the best friends necklace. I was so busy with this depressing scenario that I only half-noticed when Mr. Kelso started reading off names. And then I heard him say my name.

"..and Cathy Ferris, your partner will be Brett Roberts."

I sat up like I'd just been zapped by lightning. What was he talking about?

"What's that?" I whispered to Brianna, who was sitting next to me.

"Lucky you," she said. "You get to be partners with Brett for back-to-school night."

Oh, great. That was all I needed. A week earlier, I'd have died for the chance to be partners for anything with Brett. But that was before he'd spread it all over school that I'd nearly killed his dog, before I'd realized he was The Insensitive Jock Type. I mean, The Blabbermouth Type.

Boys are not worth it. Stay away from all types.

I made a mental note to write that in my notebook later, and then I tried to concentrate on what we were supposed to do for our project, which wasn't easy because Mr. Kelso had us move next to our partners to start discussing our projects for back-to-school night. We were to choose a topic on interpersonal relations and put together an exhibit.

Back-to-school night is always held about a month or so into the school year. It's a chance for all the parents to come in and meet the teachers. The students give reports and discuss the projects they've done.

"Okay, so what are we going to do?" asked Brett in a serious, no-nonsense voice.

"I don't know," I muttered. It was plain to see that he didn't like being with me any more than I liked being with him.

"You'd better think of something."

Why did I have to be the one to come up with a topic? That was the problem with being a former brain. Everyone expects you to come up with all the ideas.

Just then, Sherri, who was sitting in front of us, turned around. She drummed her fingers on my desk to get our attention.

"Cathy, would you mind changing partners with me? I think you and Wendall would get along so well," she said sweetly, giving Brett the full benefit of her wide smile.

Wendall looked down at the floor, obviously disappointed. I felt myself grow hot with anger. I mean, sure Brett was making me crazy, but that didn't mean I wanted to give him up to Sherri. And I didn't think it was fair for her to hurt Wendall's feelings. *Wait until I tell Jenny about this*, I thought. There was no question that Sherri was The Jerk Type.

"I think you and Wendall would make a

great team," I pointed out. My mind started working furiously. "Wendall, don't you think you and Sherri could work on how computers are affecting interpersonal relations all over the world or something? I mean, Sherri, since your dad owns Supersoft Computers and all."

Even to me, I sounded like the world's biggest phony—like I really cared about Sherri Shepherd's project.

Wendall's face lighted up like a pinball machine on tilt. "Your dad owns Supersoft Computers?"

Wendall looked at Sherri with new respect. Sherri glared at me. She was doomed. We could hear Wendall warming up to the subject, and Sherri didn't say a word.

Brett and I didn't come up with an idea for our project that day. And I knew I'd better come up with something good, or I could say good-bye to any chance for a passing social studies grade.

So, now the would-be, world-famous author had another problem to add to the pile. At the rate my problem pile was growing, it would probably reach the moon in no time!

Five

THE following Saturday was hairy—literally. Jenny and I washed so many dogs that we almost lost count. I guess it was because it was unusually warm for fall, and fleas can get pretty bad by the beach. We ran out of flea shampoo right after lunch and closed up shop. We headed to the grocery store to buy more flea shampoo for the next weekend.

"Wait," Jenny said as we pedaled our bikes past a mailbox on Peninsula Boulevard. "I have to mail this," she said, waving an envelope. "There," she said happily as she leaned her bike against the box and dropped the envelope into the slot. "That ought to help those hungry people. And I still have some money left."

I nodded my head, but I was kind of embarrassed to say anything. I mean, after all, I hadn't done anything for the hungry people. I'd spent my money paying back people I owed.

After we pedaled back from the store, we hung out in my room and watched an old beach party movie on the TV I'd taken from my parents' bedroom. Amy had gone out to play with one of her dorky little friends, so at least she wasn't around to bug us.

"I can't stay long," Jenny said. "Brianna asked me to come help her with her homework this afternoon."

"Oh," I mumbled. There it was again—that little stab I always felt whenever Jenny wanted to do something with Brianna. "Why doesn't she get someone else to help her?" I snapped.

What I really wanted to do was cry out, *What's the matter? Why do you want to be with Brianna instead of me?*

Jenny looked at me, but I couldn't tell what she was thinking.

"Don't be angry," she said softly.

"Who's angry?" I asked swiftly to hide my hurt. I fingered my half of the best friend necklace. "Shhh. The movie's starting."

We watched the movie, which was a love story about a guy who enters a surfing contest and his girlfriend. He's all set to win when his girlfriend unexpectedly enters the contest at the last minute.

"So, have you and Brett decided on your project?" Jenny asked suddenly during a commercial.

I shook my head. Then I stuck my finger in my mouth and made a gagging noise. "That's what I think of social studies and my project."

"I don't believe you," Jenny said, tossing a pillow at me. "Most girls would die to have Brett as a partner for something like this. You act like it's the worst thing that's ever happened to you. And you don't seem to be the least bit worried about your grades."

"I am worried about my grades," I said irritably. "It's just that I want to be sure we do the right project and not just jump into any old thing."

"Well, anyway, you're lucky," Jenny said. "I wish I could be assigned as a partner—for any project—with Curt. I think I'd like to write up an experiment about being stranded on a desert island with him, like Swiss Family Robinson or something."

I turned to look at Jenny. There was something soft and dreamy in her eyes. It was something that seemed to say, "Cathy, keep out." I rolled over onto my stomach and stuffed the pillow Jenny had tossed to me under my chin.

"Jenny, do you think that liking boys

changes people?" I asked slowly. My mind was working again.

Jenny looked at me in surprise. "What do you mean?"

"Oh, I don't know."

"People change all the time," she said softly. "Do you really ever know someone?"

"That's very philo—philosolop—"

"You mean philosophical. Anyway, we've been boy crazy for at least six months, and it hasn't changed us a bit," Jenny stated firmly. "Now, shhh. The movie's coming back on."

I turned back to the movie, but I closed my eyes and thought about what Jenny had said. I was envisioning her on a desert island with Curt. But in my daydream Curt suddenly changed into a snake. Then Brianna stepped into the daydream. She changed into a snake, too. Maybe it was because snakes are sneaky. I'd heard somewhere that snakes take stuff that doesn't belong to them.

After the movie ended, Jenny left to go to Brianna's. I sat in my room and tried to work on my homework. First I chewed on my pencil for a while. And then I switched to chewing my nails. That didn't exactly help me get my homework done. I finally gave up on it and threw myself on the safari comforter on my bed and tried to think of a topic for our social studies project.

Interpersonal relations. Who do I have interpersonal relations with? Mom? Dad? Jenny? Amy? No, Amy doesn't count. She's just my little sister. I'm stuck with her.

Without warning, Amy came whirling into my room to tell me about something, and she instantly knocked my ceramic elephant lamp over.

"You creep!" I shouted. "You're supposed to knock before you come in here! And look what you've done! If it's broken, you're dead meat!"

"Oh, it's not broken," Amy said, giving the lamp a light kick just to make me angry. "Anyway, Mom says you're not supposed to say 'dead meat.' She says it sounds unladylike."

"Get out!" I shouted, rising off my bed, prepared to show Amy how unladylike I could be.

"You never want to do anything with me anymore," she said, giving me a puppy-dog look.

I looked away as she left my room.

Why did Amy keep bothering me? Couldn't she see that I wanted nothing to do with her? And the more she pushed, the more I pulled away. How was that for interpersonal relations?

The next day, I slid into my seat in social studies class, and I scrunched down really low. I was hoping that somehow Brett would think I wasn't there or something, and he wouldn't come over to bug me about our project topic. I tried not to look up as he walked into the classroom. I failed. He gave me a drop-dead grin and, after tossing his book bag on his desk, came right over to my desk.

"Okay. This is it. This is the last day we can give Mr. Kelso our project topics," he said.

Suddenly, he looked right into my eyes. "Hey, are you wearing your hair differently or something? It looks good," he said.

I forced myself to look away from those eyes and to come out of my scrunch. I was in danger of falling in like again with Brett and letting him make me crazy. I couldn't afford to let that happen. Then again, I also couldn't afford not to pass social studies.

"Uh, thanks. I did try to come up with some ideas last night. Did you?" I asked, trying to force the ball back into his court.

"I've thought about the project a lot," Brett said. "I guess the best topic idea I could think of was doing something on brothers and sisters. I have a little brother. And I know that you have a little sister because I saw her when I brought my dogs over to your house to be washed. We could do our project on our little brothers and sisters and their place in the family."

Brett sat backward on a chair and looked intently at me. It was plain that he thought this was the greatest idea in the history of the world. I couldn't believe it. Do a project on Amy? Pu-leeze!

"That is the weirdest idea in the history of the world," I said. "I mean, you don't know Amy. Talk about a geek supremo."

"Well, my brother's kind of different—" Brett said softly.

"You haven't met *different* until you've met Amy," I said, rolling my eyes. "Does your brother come crashing into your room every five minutes?" I demanded.

"Well, no," Brett smiled with this kind of secretive grin. "But I thought they'd both make good project topics. If you don't like my idea, we could do something on the relations between people on sports teams." He saw my frown and added, "Can you think of anything better?"

That did it. "Okay, we'll do our project on our retarded brothers and sisters," I said.

Brett looked at me coldly when I said that and shrugged as the tardy bell rang.

"Fine," he said. And he walked off in a hurry.

Okay, so now what did I do? Brett Roberts

had turned into The Moody Type. Maybe Brett was just as upset with me as I was with him. Oh, well, at least I had something else to write in my book about guy types.

That night, I tried to call Jenny to ask her why she thought Brett acted so cold, but her mom said that she'd gone over to Brianna's.

I grabbed my book and started writing.

The Moody Type is probably the worst kind. You never know what you said or did to make him angry. You think you're doing something nice by agreeing with him, and he stomps off. What's a girl to do?

Whew, I thought after I'd finished writing. I'd already written several chapters about boys, and I was in no danger of running out of types. It's a good thing I limited my book to guy types. Girl types would fill another whole book. There was Sherri Shepherd, The Jerk Type, and Brianna Latham, The Best-Friend Stealer Type. And then there was Jenny, The Disloyal Type. These girls could probably fill up a couple of volumes!

* * * * *

The next Saturday, Jenny's dad drove us to the mall. It was Brianna's idea.

"We haven't been there for weeks!" she had wailed after school on Friday. "You and Cathy are always washing those smelly dogs on the weekends. But, look. It's raining like crazy and it's supposed to keep up all weekend. I don't see how you can wash dogs tomorrow."

She'd been right. So, there we were, in front of the Beach City Mall.

"Remember, girls," Jenny's dad said as his car splashed up to the curb in front of Tres Chic Juniors, Brianna's mom's boutique, "this mall gets crazy on Saturdays. I don't want to have to park the car to come in and find you later. Be sure you meet me here right at noon."

"Okay," we all said as we scrambled out of the car into the puddly parking lot.

We ducked inside the store and walked past the perfume counters. I managed to sidestep a salesclerk who was ready to spray me with some fragrance called Promises, Promises. She managed to spray Jenny, who can never pass up anything that's free.

"Mmm. Smell this," said Jenny as she held out her wrist.

"Yuck," I said. "Come on. We have to hurry. I want to stop at the music store and the pet store while we're here. And we don't have much time."

Of course, Brianna made a big deal out of sniffing Jenny's wrist. Pu-leeze. It was enough to make me sick.

We rode the escalator up to the juniors

department and wandered around the racks of clothes. We watched the videos on the TV overhead. I mentally bought about every third outfit—even if it was Brianna's mom's store. I had to admit that Brianna's mom knew what she was doing. I really love clothes. It's a good thing we have to wear uniforms at Tanglewood. My parents couldn't afford to buy me the clothes I would want for school.

"Oh, look," breathed Jenny. "Aren't these perfect?"

She held up a pair of jeans that had little zippers all over them.

"I thought you'd like those," Brianna said triumphantly.

I glared at her. Okay, so they're cute. *But do you have to act like you own Jenny?* I silently asked Brianna.

Jenny needed no urging to try on the jeans. They were perfect. They made Jenny look great.

"I'll take them," she said to the salesclerk. "But can I wear them out of the store?"

The salesclerk didn't seem to like the idea a whole lot, but she knew Brianna was the owner's daughter.

"Jenny's meeting her boyfriend," I said mischievously. Then I pretended I was writing a romance novel. "She and Curt have been separated for three long weeks. You see, he's been on a sailboat, and—"

"Is it okay?" Jenny interrupted, glaring at me.

It was too bad she didn't let me finish. The story was just getting good. *Maybe I'll write romance novels one day*, I thought.

"That's fine," the salesclerk said. "Just let me ring up those jeans and cut off the inventory tag. I wouldn't want anyone to think you girls were shoplifting."

I glared at her. Why did everyone think that all teenagers were shoplifters?

After we left the store, Jenny turned to me.

"Why did you start all that stuff about me and Curt?" she demanded.

"I was so embarrassed," Brianna said.

"Oh, don't get upset," I said to Jenny, ignoring Brianna like she didn't exist. Wow, sometimes Jenny sure could be The Touchy Type. "I was just trying to distract her so she'd let you wear those jeans out of the store. Aren't you happy that she let you?"

"Well—" Jenny gave in.

"The next stop is the pet store," I said, satisfied.

We walked up to the window of the pet store.

"Oh, look at the puppies," I said.

"Even through the glass, they make me sneeze," Brianna said.

I decided that Brianna is definitely The Wimpy Type.

I looked at Jenny. Instead of noticing the tiny poodle puppies in the window, she was admiring her reflection. I had to admit that she looked good. Her new jeans made her look tall and slim. I was so used to always seeing her in her gray jumper and blue blazer.

Suddenly, Curt Millikin's reflection joined ours. He was wearing a surfer T-shirt that said "Rude Shark" on it and a pair of torn-up jeans.

"Oh, hi, Curt," said Jenny, turning around and laughing a little. She lighted up like a street lamp.

"Hi, you guys," Curt said, practically looking right through Brianna and me as he continued gazing at Jenny. "Where are you guys going?" he asked after a while.

"We're on our way to the music store!" I jumped in with so much force that Jenny blinked.

"Cathy fools around on the piano," Brianna offered like it was an apology. "Every time we go to the mall, she has to go to the music store."

I started doing a slow burn.

"I don't 'fool around' on the piano," I said.

"My cousin tinkers on the piano, too," Curt said, his mouth turning up in a stupid grin.

He still didn't take his eyes off Jenny for a minute. I could have exploded all over the mall floor, and he wouldn't have noticed.

I decided that Curt is The Rude Type.

I walked ahead with Brianna, trailing while Curt and Jenny fell in behind us. When we got to the music store, I purposely walked over to one of the keyboards that was on display and plunked out "Twinkle, Twinkle, Little Star" off-key.

"Oh, you play better than that," Jenny said brightly. She was like a windup doll performing for Curt.

Just then a fat salesman, The Jovial Type, came over to where we were and started a polka on one of the electronic keyboards. Ugh.

"May I help you with something?" he asked between bouncy measures.

"Uh, no," I muttered. Out of the corner of my eye, I saw Jenny sit down with Curt on a piano bench. Brianna was watching them, too. Suddenly, the store phone rang.

"Take over for me, will you?" the salesman asked me, pointing to the keyboard.

"Yeah, sure," I said.

I took one look at that polka sheet music on the keyboard and said, "Oh, pu-leeze," shaking my head.

I closed my eyes and started playing one of my piano exercises. My fingers were stiff.

I burst forth with a rousing classical piece. I looked at Jenny and Curt. They didn't look up. I played louder. I went into a rock piece that I'd learned last year.

"That sounds great," said one of the customers in the store as he walked over to the keyboard.

I laughed. Somehow the music made me feel better. I was really getting into it. I played a new Bloated Robots tune that I'd heard on all the radio stations.

"Where did you learn to play that?" Curt asked, coming up next to me. Jenny was smiling at me. Brianna was bored—and a little upset that Jenny was paying attention to me. I felt better. And I had an audience. At least 12 people had gathered around the music store window, clapping and shouting out requests. I agreed happily to a couple of requests. I felt like a disc jockey on the radio.

Finally, Jenny tugged on my sleeve. "Come on," she hissed. "We've got to go."

I looked up and reluctantly finished my piece. People clapped and yelled, "Play some more." It was then that I noticed Curt was gone. I jumped up.

"Thanks!" the salesclerk called. Then he turned to two customers. I hoped I had helped him sell some keyboards or pianos or something.

"We're going to be late," muttered Brianna.

When we headed away from the music store, Jenny turned to me, her eyes shining. She did a funny little skip jump. "Guess what?" she burst out. "You're not going to believe this, but Curt asked me to the eighth-grade dance!"

She stopped and twirled around, waving her shopping bag that held her old pants. Her dark curls whipped merrily around her face.

"He did?" squealed Brianna.

Suddenly, something inside me melted like a glob of butter.

"That's great," I managed to utter.

It wasn't that I was jealous that Jenny had a date to the dance and I didn't. After all, that was our plan. It was something more. It was the way Curt and Jenny closed themselves in a bubble away from me—even from Brianna. It was as if, in that one little meeting in the mall, I sensed something about boys that I didn't want to have to learn about.

Boys can also be Best-Friend Stealing Types.

Six

I didn't say anything on the way home from the mall. But Jenny didn't seem to notice. She and Brianna chatted excitedly about what Jenny was going to wear to the dance. I fiddled with the electric window switch and looked straight ahead.

"I'll see you on Monday," Jenny chirped as I hopped out of the car when we got to my house.

I waved and ran up the front sidewalk, stomping furiously in the puddles.

Once I was inside the house, I took off my squishy shoes and socks and then peeled off my ski parka.

"Is that you, sweetie?" came Mom's voice.

"Yeah, it's me."

Mom came out into the hallway from the kitchen holding a bowl and stirring something with a wooden spoon.

"I'm making granola cookies," she said,

looking closely at me. "They're perfect for lifting your spirits on a rainy afternoon."

She held out the spoon for me to lick, and I licked it almost clean.

"So, are you wondering what I'm doing baking cookies like a stay-at-home mother?" she asked. Then she answered herself. "I had a few hours before my shift started, so I thought I'd whip up a batch for my two favorite girls," she said, smiling.

Then she licked the spoon herself.

"Come into the kitchen, and tell me what's on your mind," Mom said.

I followed my nose into the kitchen for a comforting chat with Mom and a few warm cookies.

"Why the long face?" she asked when I slumped at our oak kitchen table. She swirled around the kitchen dropping cookies on the sheet, checking the oven, and setting the timer.

"Jenny got asked to the eighth-grade dance," I blurted out.

"Hmm, that's nice," Mom said. "But that still doesn't explain why you're so down."

"Yes, it does!" I exploded. "Don't you see? First it was Brianna trying to take Jenny away from me. And now it's Curt."

Mom sat down at the table and looked me

in the eye. "What's this 'take away' stuff, Jenny?" she asked. "Friends aren't something that can be bought and sold, given or taken away. They aren't property you can hang 'no trespassing' signs on."

I digested that for a minute.

"Maybe not," I finally said. "But everything would have been fine, except that Jenny's surrounded by Best-Friend Stealing Types."

"Friends can't be 'stolen' either, Cathy," Mom said softly. "Sometimes people just want to explore getting to know other people—even if it means letting a best-friend relationship go on hold for a bit. And a true best friend learns to let her friend go. But she lets her know that she'll always be there for her when she's ready to come back. And, usually, the friend realizes she misses that special closeness."

My eyes started swimming with tears. I angrily wiped away the tears with my sweater sleeve.

"But, Mom, it hurts!" I wailed. "What can I do?"

Mom got up and hugged me. "There is something you can do. You can start plunging into the things you like to do, and do them well. You can work on being the best that you can possibly be. That will make you feel good about yourself. And, you know what? You'll find out that your happiness won't depend so much on one person."

I looked down at the floor tiles and started counting them while Mom's words sunk in.

"I don't get it," I said after a bit. "It still doesn't guarantee you'll get your best friend back."

"Well, that's true," Mom said mysteriously. "Oops. There's the timer."

I still wanted to pursue this subject, but the front door slammed, and Amy came crashing into the kitchen like a hurricane. She was soaking wet. Shaking herself off, she tromped over to the oven, and puddles of water formed at her feet.

"Yum. Are you baking cookies?" she asked, her nose twitching like a puppy's.

"Yes, dear," Mom answered. "Now go take off your wet things, and you can have some cookies when this first batch cools."

She winced as Amy slipped on the tile, grabbed at the counter for support, and narrowly missed slam-dunking a ceramic flour canister into my lap. I caught it neatly and placed it back up on the counter.

"You klutz!" I shouted at Amy. "You almost broke that stupid thing."

Amy stuck her tongue out at me, turned,

and clomped out of the room.

"Now, Cathy," Mom said. "Go easy on her. You know, she just does those things to get your attention. She has feelings, too."

"She's just Amy. That's her trouble," I grumbled. "Everywhere she goes, disaster follows. How am I supposed to do a decent report on her?"

"You're doing a report on Amy?" she asked.

"Oh, my social studies class is doing a section on interpersonal relations. I got stuck with Brett Roberts as a partner. He wants to do our project for back-to-school night on our brothers and sisters. It sounds dumb, huh?" I asked, reaching for a hot cookie.

"Brett Roberts is your partner?" asked Amy, returning to the kitchen. "Oh, kissy, kissy, kissy."

Ignoring Mom's warning glance, I grabbed two cookies, yanked on Amy's wet pigtail, and ran out of the kitchen. I was losing my best friend. I was stuck doing a project that was going to doom me to a failing grade. And still my little brat of a sister never let up for a minute.

Okay, so it wasn't bad enough that I had to work with Brett Roberts and that we were doing a report on a repulsive subject like brothers and sisters. Little did I realize that

70

the hardest part was yet to come.

Trying to get Brett to work on our project was worse than trying to give Bongo a bath. Here I'd made up my mind to follow Mom's advice and start picking up my grades to feel better about myself, and now it seemed Brett was going to see to it that I failed social studies.

The following Monday, I got to social studies early, hoping to talk with Brett about how we'd start our project. Brett didn't show up until just as the tardy bell rang. Then he took off right after class, without giving me a chance to ask him anything.

A couple of days later, Mr. Kelso said we were to turn in the outlines for our projects in two days. Brett gave me a thumbs-up when I looked over at him, but he took off again right as the bell rang when class was over.

"I've got practice," he said, rushing past me. "I have to go." The next day, I moved more quickly. The minute the bell rang, I shot out of my seat and headed toward Brett's desk. But I wasn't quick enough. Brett tore out of his seat, out the door, and down the hall before I had even made it to his desk.

I walked out into the hall and looked for him, but it was impossible to pick him out from the zillions of other blue blazers. Walking to my locker, I did a slow sizzle.

"Oh, hi, Cathy," came Jenny's voice from behind me.

I turned around. "Hi," I said.

"Hey, you weren't in the car pool the last couple of days. Mom said you were walking instead. How come?" she asked.

"Oh, it's nothing," I said lightly. If she wasn't going to act like anything was wrong, I wasn't going to either. And if it was going to take her a few days to notice that I wasn't around, fine. "I just felt like walking."

"Oh," Jenny said, falling in step beside me. "And did you feel like skipping lunch for two days as well? Where have you been? I've been wanting to tell you about what I'm wearing to the dance. Brianna helped me pick out the outfit."

I looked at my shoes and thought about what Mom had said about letting go.

"That's great," I said with a forced smile. But that's all I could get out.

Jenny cocked an eyebrow. "Well, I'll see you after school," she said.

I shrugged. "Okay."

We talked about everything and nothing in the car on the way home. So, Jenny and I didn't really have a chance to talk about anything.

When I got home, I went to my room and tried to write in my notebook, but then gave up. I was just too depressed to write. I grabbed my parka and walked down to the beach. The waves were gray and angry, and the stretch of sand was practically deserted.

A few lifeguard stations away, I could see a dark-haired guy. He was standing behind someone in a wheelchair. When I squinted my eyes, I could see a vague resemblance to Brett. But no, Brett would never do anything as nice as taking someone in a wheelchair to the beach. All he thinks about is sports. And I was wasting entirely too much time thinking about him.

That night, I still felt low. I didn't feel like calling Jenny, although she normally would have been just the person to cheer me up. I thought about what Mom had said again and how I was supposed to work at trying to be the best I could while my best friend was out "exploring."

Okay. The first thing to do was to work at getting my grades up. Well, that's what I was trying to do in social studies, and Brett was blowing it for me. Why did I have to wait for Brett to take time out from his stupid athletics practice to work on our project? I could do it without him.

Then I got angry. I mean, why should I do the project and he get half the credit? I thought about calling him. But even though I found his number in the phone book, I couldn't get up the nerve to dial his number. I'd never called a boy before.

I put down the phone book and picked up my notebook instead. Then, taking out a fresh sheet of paper and a pencil, I titled the paper, "Siblings." That's what brothers and sisters are called. Then I looked at the sheet for a long time, but I couldn't think of anything to write. And I wondered why. After all, Amy and I are sisters, aren't we?

I thought about that for a few minutes, and then I wandered into Amy's room. She was lying on the floor reading a book, with her legs going up the wall. There were teddy bears everywhere. Her room looked like a teddy bear factory. "Hi," I said.

Amy slid her legs down the wall and looked up at me in surprise.

"Hi," she said. "What are you doing in here?"

"I just wanted to talk," I said casually. I hadn't ventured into her room in a long time.

"You want to borrow something, right?" she asked suspiciously.

"No, I don't want to borrow anything," I

said, sitting down on a pillow on her floor. "I just wanted to hang out with you. Is that okay?"

Amy put down her book and sat with her knees tucked up under her chin. She pulled her T-shirt down toward her ankles and sat there eyeing me.

"So, what's new?" I asked, feeling weird. This talking to your sister stuff was tougher than I'd thought it would be.

"You really want to know?" Amy asked.

"Yeah," I said.

Amy smiled this great big goofy smile. "Well, today, I got picked to be the team captain for soccer, and Mrs. Presley gave me a scratch 'n sniff sticker because I did a good job on my spelling test. And Kiki Johnson hates me and says she isn't ever speaking to me again. And that's all," Amy said in a rush.

Kiki Johnson had been Amy's best friend since school started a month or so ago. Personally, I thought Kiki was The Whiney Type.

"Why isn't Kiki speaking to you?" I asked, surprised at myself that I was angry with Kiki for hating my little sister.

"She won't talk to me because I got chosen to be team captain, and she wanted to be captain," Amy said.

"Well, didn't the coach choose the team captain?" I asked. "Why should Kiki get all upset with you about it?"

Amy shrugged her thin little shoulders. "I don't know. Friends are weird sometimes. But she'll get over it by tomorrow, and we'll be best friends again." I fingered my best friend necklace and watched Amy for a minute before I got up to leave. *It sure is easy being a kid*, I thought. You can get upset with your best friend and get over it in a split second.

I went back to my room and tried to write about Amy, but nothing came to mind. So, I decided to put away my papers and work on my types book instead. I couldn't think of a single word to write. I was thinking about Amy, The Little Kid Type. Well, why not?

Watch out for The Little Kid Types. They do weird things like steal your best blouses and spill stuff on them. And they can have allergies so you can't ever have a dog. They bug you all the time and say dumb things like "kissy, kissy, kissy" when you tell your mother about The Unreliable Type. But what's funny is that sometimes they say stuff that actually makes sense.

I closed my book and went downstairs to say good night to Mom and Dad. Then I went back upstairs and crawled under my covers and worried. I worried about losing Jenny. I worried about getting my social studies project done. Then, before I fell asleep, I devoted a full five minutes to worrying about being transferred to another school.

The next day, I rode in the car pool, but I managed to sit between Brianna and the door so that Jenny and I didn't have to do more than say "hi" to each other.

As soon as we got to school, I saw Curt waiting at the curb for Jenny. That took care of any discussion I might have had with Jenny.

She waved cheerily and walked away with Curt.

I watched Brianna's sad, droopy face with a nasty little jab of satisfaction. Maybe I couldn't have Jenny to myself, but neither could Brianna.

Later that day, I stood just inside the door and waited for Brett. I was going to discuss our project if it killed me.

He came in just as the bell rang again.

"Hey, Brett," I said, grabbing his sleeve so there was no escape. The bell was still ringing. "Let's get together on our project after school today. We have to get started."

Brett looked at me blankly. "Huh? Oh, I can't work on that thing this week. I'm, uh, busy with other things."

77

"How busy can you be?" I asked. "I'm busy, too. Look, I already started working on the project. I interviewed my sister about the soccer team last night," I babbled. I didn't tell him that doing the interview had accomplished exactly nothing.

"Oh, your sister plays soccer?" Brett asked brightly, really looking at me for the first time.

Oh, boy, I groaned to myself. We're talking sports again. *Well, whatever it takes to get Brett talking,* I thought.

"Yeah," I said. "She's the team captain. She's a really good player." I had no idea if she played well or not. I'd have to ask her. "We have to work on our project this afternoon."

"I can't today," Brett muttered. "I've got something important to do."

"What could be more important than our social studies project that's due in less than two weeks?" I exclaimed. "And our outline is due tomorrow."

"I've got practice. The coach expects me to be there," Brett said.

I thrust my outline at him. "You're unbelievable," I said. Once again, Brett inspired me to write another chapter in my book. This one would be about The Impossible Type!

Seven

I was setting the table that evening when
Amy came home. And for once, she didn't
stomp. She walked in so quietly that I almost
didn't hear her.

"Hi," she said. Then she leaned up against
the counter and sighed a dramatic sigh.

"What's bugging you?" I asked as I filled
up the water glasses at the sink.

"Oh, Kiki still isn't speaking to me," Amy
said lightly. "But I don't care. I'm not talking
to her, anyway." At that, her eyes filled with
tears. She sure didn't look like someone who
didn't want to talk to her best friend.

"Don't cry," I said, setting down the water
glasses on the table and putting my arm
around her.

Amy sniffled and huddled into my shoulder.

I wished I could think of something to say

to make her feel better.

"You know," I began slowly, searching for words. "Maybe you need to let Kiki work this out for herself. Let her know that you'll be there for her when she's ready to be your friend. And in the meantime, you should just concentrate on your soccer and being a good sport. You've got to feel good about yourself."

Where had I heard those words before?

Amy pulled away from me and rolled her eyes at me. "What do you know?" she muttered.

I laughed sadly. "Not too much," I admitted. "But I just want you to feel better."

"Well, thanks," she said. Then she shocked me to death. She came over and hugged me. So, I hugged her back.

That's how we were when Mom and Dad walked into the kitchen. They beamed at us until I thought I was going to barf.

"What, you're not fighting?" asked Dad. He widened his eyes and pretended to gasp with shock.

"I like to see you two getting along," Mom said with an ear-to-ear grin.

"Don't expect it to last," Amy said gruffly. But she winked at me when no one was looking. And I winked back.

"How about after dinner we catch that new

sci-fi movie that's playing downtown?" Dad asked suddenly.

We both looked up at him in surprise. Normally, we never go out on a school night. School nights are reserved for homework. Period.

"All right!" exclaimed Amy.

"After I finish my homework," I said.

Mom looked extra pleased at my comment.

The movie was great. But the best part was being able to forget about Brett and our stalled social studies project. And being able to forget about Jenny and our stalled friendship was good, too. Instead, I only had to worry for an hour and a half about whether the hero would be able to rescue the heroine and save the universe from the forces of the black void.

He did, and we walked out of the theater completely satisfied.

The next evening, we went out for dinner at a Chinese restaurant. When we got home, Dad replayed the telephone answering machine. I didn't pay any attention to it—that is, until I heard a deep voice saying, "Hi, Cathy. This is Brett. Call me tonight if it's not too late at 555-4769."

I think I stopped breathing for a second.

"Oh, he must be calling me about my outline," I said.

It's about time, I thought.

Amy raised and lowered her eyebrows exaggeratedly about three times and said, "Wooo-wooo" with a little wiggle of her hips.

I sighed. She was back to being Amy, public enemy number one.

"Is it too late to call?" I asked Dad eagerly.

"Go ahead. But make it short," Dad said.

I went upstairs and pulled the phone into my room from the hall. I went over to the door and locked it so Amy couldn't come in.

I took a deep breath, but just as I went to pick up the phone, it rang.

"Hello?" I answered.

"Hi, Cathy. It's me, Jenny."

"Oh, hi," I said with a sigh.

"What are you doing?" she asked.

"Oh," I lied, "I'm working on my surefire best-seller." I didn't want Jenny to know that Brett had called. And I certainly didn't want her to think that I was pining away for her. Because I wasn't.

"In fact," I went on, "I just finished the chapter on The Impossible Type. Just wait until this book hits the stores. I'll be rich and famous!"

"Being rich and famous won't do much for your love life," Jenny pointed out.

I couldn't believe it. Was she going to act

all great because she had a date for the dance and I didn't? I hung up on her.

The phone rang again just as Amy started pounding on the door and yelling, "Open up! It's against the rules to lock your door!"

I unlocked the door and glared murderously at my sister, and then I dashed for the phone.

"I'll have you know it'll do wonders for my love life!" I shouted into the receiver.

"What's going to do wonders for your love life?" asked a deep, masculine voice.

It wasn't Jenny! I wanted to die. I squeaked out, "This isn't Jenny?"

"Uh, no, It's Brett—Brett Roberts."

I could see my face in the dresser mirror. It's amazing how I could turn several shades of red all at the same time. It was technicolor embarrassment.

"Just forget what I said. It was a joke—a bad one," I said lamely, while dodging my sister who was standing over me trying to make kissing noises. I jammed my hand over her mouth. She pushed it away.

"Okay. Consider it forgotten," Brett replied. "I wanted to talk to you about the outline. I had a little time to work on it. I didn't do much to it, but I'll show it to you tomorrow before we turn it in."

"Okay," I said as I reached to tug on Amy's

pigtail since it was within range.

Brett made some small talk about Tanglewood's football team (what else?), which I only half-heard because my hand was over the receiver as I hissed dire threats at Amy.

"I'm sorry that it took me so long to start working on the project, but I've been busy with..." Brett said just as Amy tripped over the phone cord.

"...and I wanted to explain it to you."

"You are dead!" I whispered furiously at Amy. "Get out of my room!"

"...and I'd like to ask you if you would come with me. It's kind of different..." Brett's voice was lost as Amy's foot got caught in the cord. She fell heavily against my desk, sending my books crashing down, followed shortly by my elephant lamp. This time it broke all over the place. I grabbed Amy by the arm and propelled her through the door. Then I shut if firmly and locked it—rules or no rules.

I returned to the phone. "That sounds interesting. I'd love to go. When did you say it was? Saturday afternoon? Okay."

When Brett hung up, I jumped up and down. He'd asked me out. And what's more, he'd worked on the outline. There was hope. Even if most of my interpersonal relations were the pits, maybe at least I wouldn't flunk out of Tanglewood.

"So, I'm going out with him. Of course, I really just want to get more information for my book. Brett's still one of those guys to beware of," I explained to Jenny the next day as soon as we got out of the car.

I was so excited that I didn't even care if Brianna heard everything.

"Of course," said Jenny, holding back a smile that I chose to ignore. "So, where's he taking you? Is he taking you to the dance?"

I wrinkled my nose, but decided to let Jenny's comment about the dance pass. She probably wasn't trying to rub it in.

"Actually, I'm not too sure," I confessed. "Amy chose that particular moment to stage a tornado in my bedroom, so I didn't hear everything Brett said. But you know his type. He's probably taking me to some sort of sporting event."

"You might be surprised," Jenny murmured.

I smiled at her and shrugged my shoulders. Whatever she thought, it was good to be talking with her again. And it didn't even bother me when Curt came up to us and walked with us for a while. I was thinking about Brett so much that it didn't even bother me that I was sharing Jenny.

I wasn't surprised to find out how difficult it was to concentrate on schoolwork that day. But I really tried. I didn't daydream about my book or the clothes I was going to buy when I was rich and famous. Now that I was going to ace social studies, I might as well bring up my other grades.

I somehow survived the morning and made it to social studies. This time, I didn't have to wait for Brett. He met me at the door.

"Here's the outline for the project," he said, handing it to me. He acted all calm, not like he'd asked me out for a date just the night before. "You can do whatever you like with it. Look it over. We don't have to turn it in until the end of class."

I took it hurriedly, not trusting myself to talk to him, and rushed to my seat. My heart thumped wildly as I watched Brett's blue blazer as he sat down.

While Mr. Kelso showed a film, I looked over the outline. It was great! I made a couple of little changes here and there, but it was pretty good. Okay. So, maybe I'd have to fix up the chapter in my book about how stupid jocks are.

I got Sherri to tap Brett on his shoulder, and I gave him the thumbs-up sign. He gave me a killer grin, and then he turned around. Maybe I'd have to dump the entire chapter on The Insensitive Jock Type.

As soon as class was over, I jumped up and placed our outline on Mr. Kelso's desk. Then I turned to look for Brett. I wanted to ask him where we were going for our date. But he was talking with Sherri. Something he said made her throw back her wavy blond hair and laugh like a screeching chimpanzee. She gave me a triumphant look before turning back to him. They walked out of class together, their blue shoulders touching.

My stomach almost staged a Brett Rebellion. I stood there for a minute until someone pushed past me. That reminded me that I'd better hurry if I didn't want to miss the car pool.

The next day, we played touch football in gym class. It was the blue team against the red team. "What are you worried about? He asked you out, not Sherri," Jenny asked between gasps for air.

"Who's worried?" I asked as we got in formation, ready to launch our offensive play.

Jenny stood up, wiped some mud from her cheek, and hooted.

"Don't try to fool me. If you weren't worried, why did you try to tackle Sherri just now?

You know the rules. We're only supposed to yank off our opponents' flags. You're lucky Coach Palmer didn't see you."

"Well, who cares about Brett, anyway?" I muttered. He's the type who asks someone out for a date and then flirts with the next girl who comes along. It just so happens that he's the inspiration for chapter one: The Athletic Type: Run, Swim, Jump—But Keep-Away's The Best Game To Play With This Type." I closed my eyes as I envisioned the illustration for this particular chapter.

"Hey, Jen!" I'd suddenly had a flash of brilliance. How'd you like to illustrate my book? Your drawings are killer!"

I never did hear her answer on that one because just then I intercepted a pass with my stomach. The next thing I knew, my teammates were carrying me from the muddy field in questionable glory. I spent the next few minutes trying to catch my breath and convince Coach Palmer that I was okay.

It wasn't until later, after we'd all taken showers, that I was able to continue trying to convince Jenny of the genius of my book. I kept getting interrupted, though, by Sherri, who was telling everyone within hearing distance about her football injuries—two tiny bruises to be exact.

After school, while Jenny and I were waiting for the car pool, I started my campaign again.

"Forget it," Jenny said. "You really shouldn't be working on a book right now. You need to get your grades up."

"They are going up. I just turned in the world's greatest outline for social studies." I started.

"And have you figured out what you're going to wear for your date with Brett?" Jenny asked.

I stopped and sighed.

"Let's go to the mall and pick out an outfit for you!" squealed Brianna suddenly.

I eyed her for a moment. Was she just agreeing with Jenny? Or did she care about what I was going to wear on my first date? But just as suddenly, it didn't matter that much anymore.

I surprised myself. "That would be great."

Okay. So, not only was I bringing up my grades to feel better about myself, but I was also learning to share. And guess what? Mom was right. It did make me feel good.

The good feeling lasted until just before dinner when I called Jenny to see if she'd finished her homework yet.

Her mom, Gail, answered.

"Oh, she and Brianna went to a homecoming committee meeting," she said.

My shoulders slumped. Jenny had never told me she was going to be on the homecoming committee with Brianna. And she'd never even asked me to be on it. Maybe Mom was wrong. This sharing your best friend stuff was for the birds.

I went to my room, turned on my radio, and let the music swirl around my head. Hugging my stuffed giraffe, I sat quietly, listening to the faint crashing of the waves outside.

Suddenly, a knock came at my door. I could hear Amy's sniffly breathing.

"What do you want?" I grumbled.

She let herself into my room. "I just want to talk," she said.

"You creep! Do you really think I'm talking to you?" I snapped.

"Now what did I do?" she asked.

"Remember last night? Remember when I was trying to talk on the phone, and you started a riot in my room?" I asked.

Amy looked at me. "That's okay," she said quietly. "I knew you didn't really mean it when you started being nice to me."

Eight

THINGS didn't get any better in the personal relations department all week. I ignored Amy. And Brett ignored me. At least, I think he did. He continued to leap from his seat right after classes every day, so I didn't know what he was thinking. I didn't see Jenny until Friday after school before my big date with Brett. She'd been involved with the homecoming committee and had even gotten to miss lots of class because of it.

Okay, fine. So, Jenny wanted to be best friends with Brianna. See if I cared. I'd tried to do it Mom's way and let Jenny go while I worked on being the best I could be. Look where it got me.

I took off my half of the best friends necklace and dumped it in a lump in my jewelry box that Grandma Ferris had given to me. I did my homework like a maniac all week and took incredible notes in class. I stuck my hand up at every question the teachers asked. I pulled two A's and a $B+$ on class quizzes.

On Thursday morning, Mr. Hogg pulled me aside after class.

"Miss Ferris," he said, his glasses sliding down his nose. "You seem to be concentrating again on your science work, and it shows."

"Uh, thanks, Mr. Hogg," I said, sort of embarrassed. I mean, I guess it wasn't that hard, if you just stick with something.

Still, I walked out of the classroom with a bright, tingly glow. Well, even though I was striking out with Jenny and Brett, I figured that at least I wouldn't get kicked out of Tanglewood. And even without Jenny around as much, it was a pretty cool school. So, I wasn't a total Loser Type.

On Friday afternoon, I walked over to meet the car pool and waited for my mom. It was her day to drive. Suddenly, someone came up behind me and clapped a pair of hands over my eyes.

"Guess who?" came a gruff voice.

I spun around to peel off the hands. It was Jenny.

"Hi," she said happily, like she hadn't been ignoring me all week. "I ditched out of the homecoming committee meeting today. You and I have something very important to do."

"What's that?" I asked.

Jenny hooted. "Did you forget? We're going to the mall today to pick out something for you to wear for your big date with Brett," she said.

"Well, I thought you'd forgotten," I said. "And what about Brianna?"

"She's with the homecoming committee."

"I didn't ask my mom if I could go to the mall."

"Well," Jenny pointed out. "She's driving the car pool today, so it's easy. We'll just ask her when she picks us up. We pass the mall on our way home, anyway. And my mom will pick us up."

"Okay," I said grudgingly. I mean, Jenny ignores me all week, and then she just waltzes back into my life like nothing happened. Oh, well. I guess it would be fun to have her help me pick out an outfit.

Just then, Mom's car turned into the drive in front of Tanglewood. I could see Amy's head barely sticking up over the dashboard.

As soon as we climbed inside the car, I piped up. "Mom, can you drop us off at the mall on the way home? Jenny's going to help me pick out an outfit to wear when I go out with Brett tomorrow."

"Did you bring your dog-washing money with you?" Mom asked.

"Oops," I said.

Mom just laughed. "All right. You can borrow some money from me until you get home."

I reached over the seat and hugged her. "Thanks, Mom."

When we got to the mall, Jenny and I went straight for Tres Chic Juniors. After browsing for a while, I held up two of the cutest sweaters for Jenny's inspection.

"Maybe I'll just get a new sweater to wear. What do you think of these?" I asked anxiously. "Which do you think Brett would like the best?"

"You know what I think?" Jenny asked with a hint of a hoot. "I don't think you're just going out with Brett to work on material for your book. I think you still really like him."

I stuck out my tongue at her. "Just tell me which color you think is best."

"You, know, I still think you're making a huge mistake writing that book, anyway," Jenny pressed.

"Which sweater would go better with my new red pants?" I avoided her comment.

Jenny sighed and pointed to the bright yellow one with a pretty cabbage rose woven into it. I placed the other sweater back on the shelf. While the salesclerk rang up the sweater, I tried to tell Jenny she was wrong about my feelings for Brett.

"You see, you just aren't as observant as I am. So, maybe you can't spot types like I can. My book will be perfect for people like you," I said. "That way, for example, you can recognize, well, people like Brianna and Curt—The Best-Friend Stealing Types." There. I'd said it.

I stood there and watched the thunderclouds gathering on Jenny's face.

"Now, don't get angry," I added. "It's the truth, and you know it."

"Is that why you've been acting so weird lately?" Jenny asked.

"I've been acting weird?" I asked so loudly that a salesclerk looked over in our direction. "Who's the one who traded in her best friend for Brianna Latham? Who's the one who joined the homecoming committee without saying a word to me?"

"Well, I knew you weren't taking on any new activities until you brought up your grades," Jenny interrupted in protest.

"Oh, sure," I said disbelievingly.

Jenny eyed me for a moment. "You know, for someone who thinks she's so observant, you should have learned something by now. You can't pin your neat little labels on people and expect them to perform exactly as you planned," she said heatedly. "By the way, you're wrong about Brianna. In case you hadn't 'observed,' she's lonely and could stand someone paying a little attention to her. But you're still my best friend, and if you'd quit being so blind, you'd figure that out."

I stood there, ready to spring back with a zingy comeback. My brain went on overload or something. I couldn't think of a thing to say.

"So, go stuff that in your book," said Jenny. She walked out of the store, leaving me to figure out how to get home from the mall by myself.

"Some people are so touchy," I grumbled as I deposited a quarter in the pay phone to call my mom. But I was smiling. After all, Jenny and I were still best friends—even if she was upset with me. But that's one thing about Jenny. She never stays angry for very long. I know her type. She'd call me up later. We'd giggle, and she'd tell me what earrings and shoes and stuff I should wear with my new outfit.

I was wrong. Jenny didn't call. Okay, so I was wrong for once. By early Saturday afternoon, I really missed Jenny—and her advice. I was getting ready to go out with Brett, and I sure could have used her help. I must have tried on at least 10 different pairs of earrings. They all looked dorky. I'd rather die than admit it, but I wanted to look extra-special for Brett. It's hard enough to look good when you know where you're going, but forget it when you don't know whether it's an indoor thing or an outdoor thing, and whether it's dressy or casual.

I gave up and applied a little lip gloss, and then I glanced at my watch. Brett was 15 minutes late. It figures. Those Athletic Types are totally inconsiderate.

Amy had just gotten back from her gymnastics lesson, and she was pestering me unmercifully. "He's late. Did he stand you up?" she teased.

"No, he didn't," I grumbled. Pushing aside that possibility, I went downstairs. I nibbled on some cookies for a while. Then I nibbled on my nails for a while. Frowning, I checked the kitchen clock. He was a half hour late. That did it!

I stomped up to my room and grabbed my notebook and trusty pen. Scribbling madly, I slashed angrily across my paper.

All Athletic Types are worthless. They

*don't have a considerate bone in their bod-
ies. They're late with everything—including
important school outlines and dates—probably because they can't bear to tear themselves
away from the mirror, checking out how great
they look. They have no consideration for
others.*

I spent my burst of annoyance and, letting
my writing hand rest for a minute, glanced
out the window just in time to see a large blue
van pull up our drive. That's funny. I'd have
thought Brett's parents would drive a sports
car or something. I watched as Brett jumped
out. He was wearing navy blue shorts and a
light blue polo shirt. He had a sweatshirt tied
around his neck. Okay. So, he looked great.

Suddenly, my eyes traveled to his running
shoes. Are we going running? I groaned to
myself and shot a glance at my red flats. My
feet hurt already.

The doorbell rang, and I slowly walked
down the stairs. I didn't want to appear too
anxious. My anger had magically evaporated
at the first sight of Brett. Amy flew down the
stairs and beat me to the door.

"Get back, creep," I hissed. I hauled her
back by the collar while I opened the door.

"Hi, Brett," I greeted him and continued
to wrestle with Amy. "Would you just back

off, you creep?"

"So, this is your little sister, the one who plays soccer?" Brett asked. His eyes softened as he looked at Amy.

Amy beamed.

"Yeah," I answered. "She's the one."

"I'm team captain because I've got the strongest kick," Amy boasted, looking up at Brett worshipfully.

Brett let out a long whistle. "Wow, you are? That's great," he said.

I was surprised. I never pegged Brett as the type who likes little kids.

"Listen, I'm sorry we were so late. Something in the electrical ramp broke, and I had to fix it. For a while, I thought we'd have to miss the race. I was worried. There'd be some really disappointed people if we weren't there," Brett said.

"No problem, I said. "I was running late, anyway." So, Brett was actually concerned that he'd kept someone waiting. He was beginning—just beginning, mind you—to mess up my theory about Self-centered Jock Types. Anyway, I was sure he'd prove me right again during the next few hours.

"Dad, I'm leaving. I'll be back by dark!" I called as I walked out the door.

"Hey, are you going to a race? Can I come,

too?" asked Amy.

"No, you can't come," I said, glaring at her.

"Well, why not? We could use a strong girl like you," Brett said. Then he gave me a wink and put his arm around me. Boy, that caught me by surprise.

I sure didn't want Amy tagging along on my first real date. But on the other hand, if Brett wanted her to come, I didn't want him to think I was a bad sport.

While she ran in to ask permission, I walked ahead with Brett.

"I hope you don't mind that I said she could come," he said. "But I think my brother would like it, and we both need to know each other's siblings for our project, anyway. The next time we go out, we won't ask her to come along."

That did it. He'd said, "the next time we go out." That was enough for me. And then I surprised myself. I decided Brett was right— and that I really didn't mind if Amy went with us.

Maybe I was learning to share.

Nine

"DO you think you'll be comfortable?" Brett asked eyeing my clothes and shoes. It was kind of hot for a fall afternoon, but since I didn't dare admit that I didn't know exactly where we were going, I just shrugged and smiled.

"I'm comfortable," Amy chipped in. She was wearing a sweat suit and sneakers.

Brett smiled in approval. It figures. He invites my little sister along on our date—and he seems to like her better.

As we walked over to the great big van, I began to get suspicious. Was this going to be a group venture? Was the next stop the boys' locker room where we were going to pick up the entire Tanglewood football team?

"That's my brother, Ryan," Brett nodded in the direction of the back of the van. "And this is my mom."

"Hi, Mrs. Roberts," I said. I'd met her before, but I wasn't sure she'd remember me. But then again, I wondered if she'd remember me as the girl who nearly got Bongo killed.

Mrs. Roberts was pretty. She had the same dark hair and the same blue eyes as Brett. She was wearing a royal blue sweat suit and matching sneakers. Her hair was pulled back in a ponytail with a white sweatband. I looked down at my sweater and jeans. I definitely was the odd girl out.

Brett opened the van door, and I climbed into the passenger seat. Brett and Amy climbed into the seats behind me. When I turned around, I think my face must have registered a complete blank. Ryan was seated in a sideways backseat. He waved happily at me, and I waved back. But I was busy staring at all the gadgets in the van. Then I looked around at Ryan's wheelchair. Finally, I looked at Ryan's legs bound in a tangle of straps.

"Say 'hi' to Cathy and Amy, Ryan," said Brett as he leaned over to snap Amy's seat belt. "Amy is the girl I told you about who plays soccer."

Ryan didn't say anything.

"Say 'hello,' Ryan," Mrs. Roberts coaxed gently. Still, Ryan didn't answer. He looked first at Amy and then at me. "Ryan's pretty excited about going to the track," Mrs. Roberts explained to me as she put the van in gear and we backed out of the driveway.

"Cathy and Amy are going with us to the track," Brett said to Ryan.

"Are we going race now?" Ryan asked anxiously. Though he looked only a year or so younger than Brett and me, his voice was like a little kid's, high and uneven.

"You bet. And we're going to be cheering you on," Brett boomed as we took off down our street. He reached up and touched my shoulder. "Aren't we, Cathy? Isn't that what big brothers and sisters are for?"

"Of course," I answered, my head spinning. We were going to watch a race. Or, were we going to be in a race? Ryan said something that I didn't hear, and I stared ahead at the road for a few minutes, not contributing anything to the chatter going on around me.

Suddenly, I felt Brett's eyes on me, and I turned to look at him. I remembered that day on the beach when I thought I'd seen Brett standing behind someone in a wheelchair. Then I remembered what I'd said about doing our social studies project on our retarded brothers and sisters. How could I have said something so stupid? I'd been The Insensitive Type. It's a good thing that Brett was

103

The Forgiving Type.

After we arrived at the Beachside College campus, we unloaded Ryan and the wheelchair at the parking lot near the track. It was slow going. The electric ramp didn't seem to be working right. But finally, the wheelchair was on the ground.

"Wow! Check this out," said Amy. She ran her hands over the sleek lines of Ryan's wheelchair. The wheels were small and thin, but they looked strong.

"It's made from special alloys and designed aerodynamically so it can really move," said Brett proudly.

"Race, race, race," Ryan said, giggling and bouncing up and down in his chair.

At first I worried that I was staring, but after a minute, I relaxed. Amy didn't seem to make a big deal out of the fact that Ryan was a special kid. Maybe I had something to learn from my little sister.

Ryan spotted a couple of kids he knew, and he started bouncing and giggling even more.

"Take it easy," Mrs. Roberts said, resting her hands on Ryan's shoulders. "Amy, why don't you come with Ryan and me while we see where we're supposed to line up. Brett, why don't you and Cathy go find out where we get our number."

"Wait until I tell Kiki about this!" Amy said excitedly.

So, Kiki and Amy are speaking to each other again, I thought.

Brett waved to the others and fell in step with me. As we walked toward a group of buildings, he reached over and grabbed my hand and gave it a squeeze. I shivered slightly, even though it was awfully hot in the sun. Watching the wheelchairs and the laughing, noisy competitors around me, I felt myself getting caught up in the excitement.

"All right, Brett Roberts," I said, turning to playfully whomp his shoulder with my free hand. "Why didn't you tell me about Ryan and all of this before?"

Brett grinned this neat grin that I was sure he'd invented especially for me. "What was there to tell? Ryan's had cerebral palsy since he was born. Mom and I have been coaching him for this race for weeks. He loves it. Of course, this is only a selection race. Then we'll see if he gets to participate in the Special Olympics."

"Wow," I said, sounding a little like Amy. "So, this is why you chose siblings for our social studies project."

"And that's why sometimes I was too busy to work on the outline," Brett said sheepishly.

He gave my hand another squeeze. "I'm sorry about that."

I squeezed back.

"Anyway, after you told me that your little sister liked sports, it just seemed like the perfect topic for us to do."

Suddenly, I felt a little ashamed. True, Amy played soccer, but I'd never gone to a single one of her games. I'd never asked her if she won or lost. I wondered if she'd noticed.

I looked up at Brett, his face shining with the excitement of his brother's upcoming competition.

"Yeah," I said. "I've got some catching up to do with Amy before we can pull our project together completely."

"This must be where we get the numbers," Brett said as we stopped in front of a booth.

While we signed in and waited for the lady at the window to give us Ryan's number, I thought about how much I suddenly understood Brett. Yes, Jenny was right. You can't pin neat little labels on people and expect them to behave in certain ways. People are too complicated for that.

And sometimes they surprise the heck out of you.

Ten

A few minutes later, Amy and I were seated with Mrs. Roberts in the front row of the bleachers. We were right by the starting line, so we could see everything—the white chalk stripes for the lanes, the faces of the kids sitting in their wheelchairs in the ready position, and the guy with the starting gun. Brett was trying not to show how nervous he felt as he finally stepped away from the back of Ryan's chair.

Amy jammed her fist in her mouth. "I can't stand this waiting," she said, removing it for a second. "I mean, imagine how excited those guys are. They've been training for months. Think of how Brett must feel. Once that gun goes off, he can't do a thing. He just has to stand there and watch. It's all up to Ryan."

I turned and smiled at Amy. For a nine year old, she can think some pretty grown-up thoughts   sometimes.

Crack! The gun went off, and the chairs shot forward. I didn't watch the race for a few seconds. Instead, I watched the look on Brett's face. It was a mixture of intense concentration, worry, and a whole lot of love. It definitely was not the face of The Insensitive Jock Type.

Hours later, the tired and triumphant Roberts boys pulled up our driveway to drop off tired and triumphant Cathy and Amy Ferris. Amy bounded ahead, while Brett walked me to the door slowly. After a long afternoon of cheering for Ryan and the other kids, we'd had a picnic under a tree and later had explored the creek that I hadn't played near since I was about six. Brett had showed Amy the place where a little pond formed, and you could see weird plants and squiggly bugs.

"I had a nice time, Cathy." Brett looked anxiously into my eyes. "I hope you did, too. Ryan thinks you and Amy are the greatest sports."

"We did have a great time," I said. "I mean it. Thank you." I really did mean it. I, Miss Sure-of-Herself, was shaken up a bit at first by the surprise of all the startling new discoveries. But I'd had a lot of fun. I'd learned a little about myself, something about Amy, something about Brett—and a lot about people. Actually, I'd learned a lot about Brett, The Ex-selfish Type.

I savored the kiss Brett planted on the tip of my nose for hours. We made a date for the next afternoon to start working on our social studies project. And best of all, my ears rang with his invitation to the eighth-grade dance!

The next morning, I called Jenny to apologize about a lot of things. She accepted my apology and forgave me, like I'd hoped she would. I put on my friends half of the best friends necklace again right before she came over. We set up the dog-washing business for a special Sunday session. We needed to earn some money to donate to the Special Olympics.

"And wait until you see the essay I wrote for back-to-school night. I was up half the night last night working on the project," I boasted to Jenny. "No more grade problems for me."

Jenny smiled and filled the tub for Brandy.

"If you could have seen how proud Brett was of his brother, and how patient he was," I continued. "Nothing slows them down. And the wheelchair races were awesome. For a while, it looked like this girl from Del Mar was going to win. But then Ryan got a burst of energy and just whizzed by her," I babbled happily. Brandy waved his tail ecstatically at my enthusiasm, spraying Jenny and me freely.

Jenny tightened her grip on the Saint Bernard while I hosed him down, and she gave me another knowing smile.

"Brett's got another side to him besides The Unfeeling, Blabbermouth, Athletic Type, huh? Maybe like Brianna has another side to her besides The Best-Friend Stealing Type? And like Curt has another side to him?" Jenny asked lightly.

"Maybe," I said. "But don't you dare say that Sherri has another side to her than The Jerk Type, or I'll barf all over the place."

Jenny shook her head. "I wouldn't go that far. I saw her flirting with Curt the other day. She's The Jerk Type, all right. But just don't go and nominate Brett for a medal just because he's a special person with a special family. You don't have room in your book for a chapter on medal-winning types," Jenny added. She didn't realize how close she was to receiving a drenching from a certain garden hose.

"Oh, I decided to trash my types book," I mentioned as nonchalantly as possible.

"You decided that I was right, that you couldn't type people?" Jenny asked, victory dripping in her voice.

"Not exactly," I answered, neatly avoiding that trap. "It's just that I have plans to write another book. The other one would have trashed my love life. And how would I ever have learned about boys?"

Lucky for her, Jenny didn't answer that one.

About the Author

KARLE DICKERSON is the managing editor of a young women's fashion and beauty magazine based in southern California. She lives with her husband and numerous animals, including a horse, a Welsh pony, three cats, a dog, and two hermit crabs.

"I first decided to be a writer when I was 10 years old and had a poem published in the local paper," she says. "I wrote almost every day in a journal from that day on. I still use some of the growing-up situations I jotted down then for my novel ideas and magazine articles."

Mrs. Dickerson spends her spare time at Stonehouse Farms, a southern California equestrian center she and her husband formed with some friends. She says, "I love to ride my horse around the ranch and people-watch. It seems this is when I come up with some of my best ideas!"